Daniel R. Cady

Memorial of Lieut. Joseph P. Burrage

A Funeral Sermon

Daniel R. Cady

Memorial of Lieut. Joseph P. Burrage
A Funeral Sermon

ISBN/EAN: 9783337116682

Printed in Europe, USA, Canada, Australia, Japan

Cover: Foto ©Raphael Reischuk / pixelio.de

More available books at **www.hansebooks.com**

Funeral Sermon.

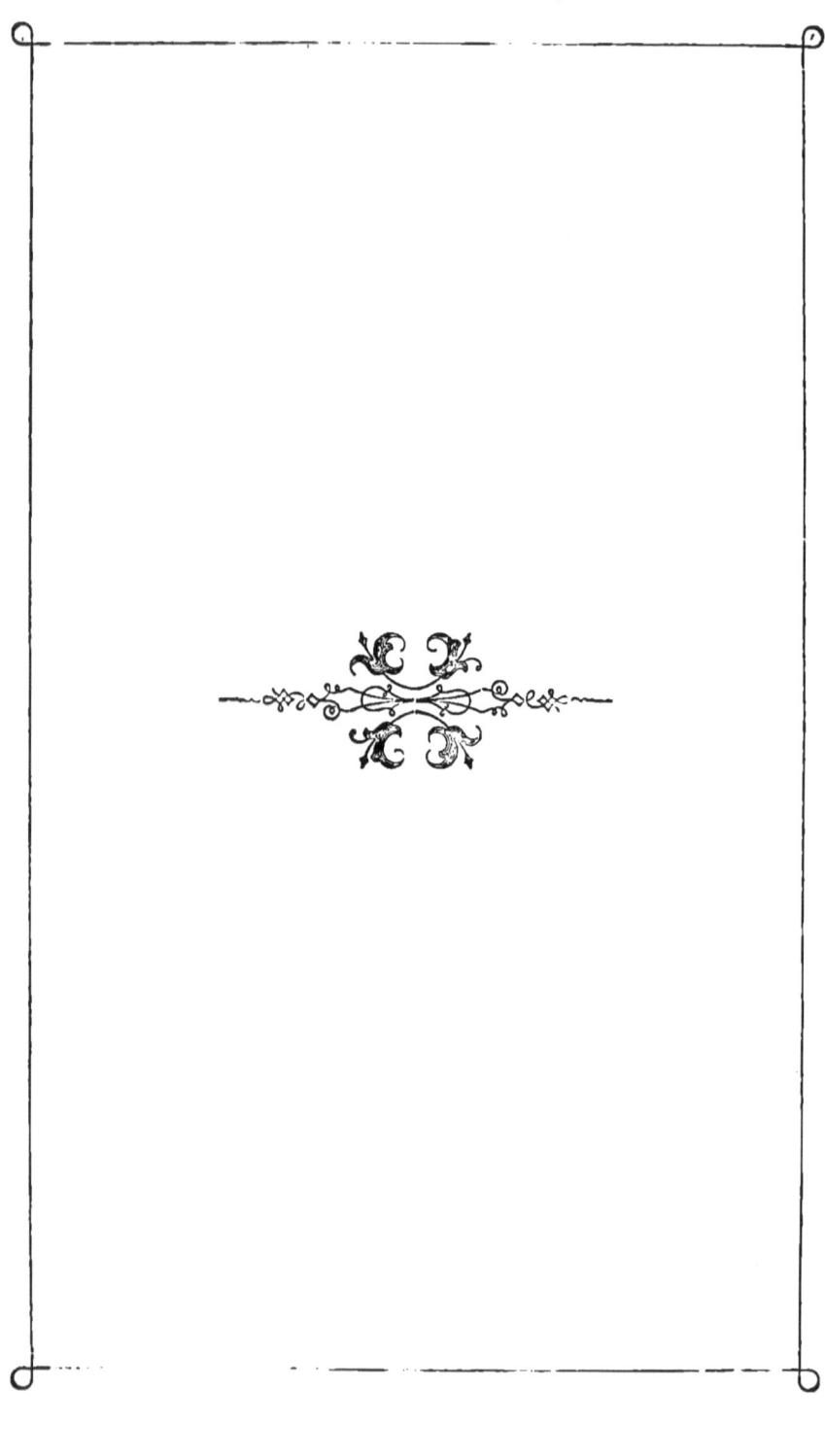

MEMORIAL

OF

LIEUT. JOSEPH P. BURRAGE:

A

Funeral Sermon,

PREACHED DECEMBER 25, 1863,

BY

REV. DANIEL R. CADY,

PASTOR OF THE ORTHODOX CHURCH, WEST CAMBRIDGE, MASS.

BOSTON:

GOULD AND LINCOLN,

59 WASHINGTON STREET.

1864.

GEO. C. RAND & AVERY,
ELECTROTYPERS AND PRINTERS.

Prefatory Note.

THE following sermon was written with no thought of its use beyond the occasion for which it was prepared. But many having expressed a wish to possess it as a permanent memorial, one who greatly loved him whom it commemorates proposed to print it for private distribution among personal friends.

For a purpose so grateful to many hearts, the generous offer could not be refused.

D. R. C.

WEST CAMBRIDGE, JAN. 25, 1864.

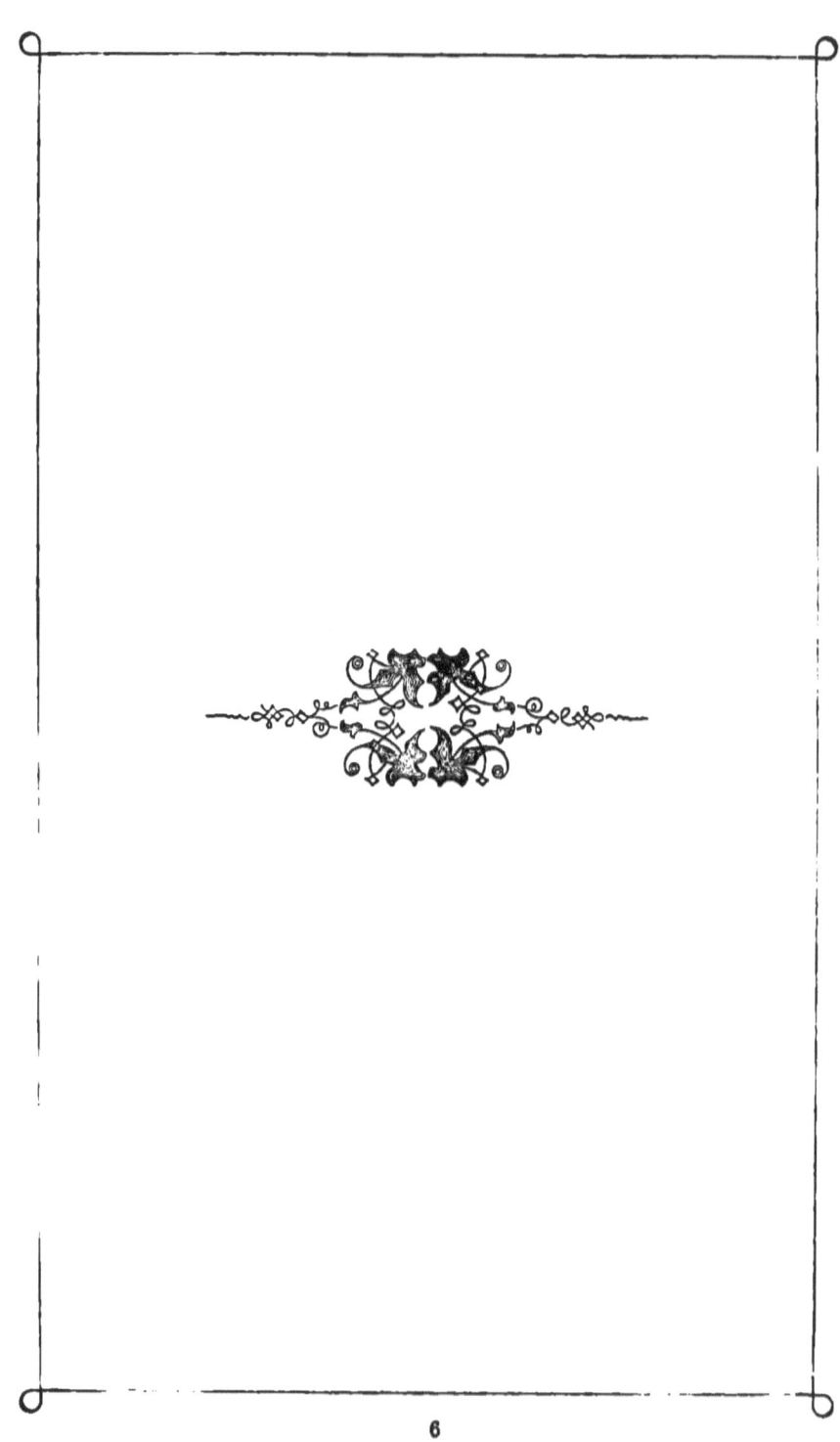

Funeral Sermon.

AND THIS IS THE VICTORY THAT OVERCOMETH THE WORLD,
EVEN OUR FAITH. — 1 John 5:4.

A MOMENTOUS truth underlies the declaration of the text. This earthly life is one of conflict. The human race has brought itself into such a moral condition that there is a constant antagonism between the apparent and

the real,— between the present and the
future,— between the indulgence of the
senses, the appetites, the passions, and
obedience to truth, conscience, God. This
is the "conflict of the ages;" the contro-
versy perpetuated from generation to
generation. Now the apostle asserts that
in this great contest, whose battle-field is
every human heart, faith alone giveth
the victory. "The world," as used here,
includes within the scope of its meaning
all evil tendencies, desires, influences;
and "faith," which is placed in contrast
with it, is an affectionate confidence in a
personal God, in his being, his character,
his government. It recognizes his law

as the rule of right to all moral beings,
and an obligation to obey it which nothing can render void. It trusts implicitly
in him, as the wise and merciful Father
and Ruler of all, and in his son Jesus
Christ, our Lord. It believes that he has
purposes of mercy toward his children
individually, and toward the race collect-
ively,—purposes which he constantly car-
ries forward, sometimes by means whose
fitness we can discover, often by those the
reasons for which we cannot understand,
and whose beneficial effects we are un-
able to trace. Yet, seen or unseen, understood or not understood, faith accepts
them all as the wise appointments of One

who cannot err, "whose ways are higher than our ways, and his thoughts than our thoughts;" and in the darkness and in the light alike, it strives to know and to do his will; and, looking upward, tries ever to say, "Even so, Father, for so it seemeth good in thy sight." Thus, in the sunshine and in the storm, in joy and in sorrow, in the hour of temptation and of trial, in times of private calamity or of public disaster, "this is the victory that overcometh the world, even our faith."

Emergencies often occur in our personal experience and in the history of nations, when nothing but an unwavering confidence in the truth, an unshaken trust in divine Providence, an unfaltering belief in the final triumph of right, will sustain the heart and nerve the arm for duty.

Appetite and passion beset the young and tempt them to idleness, to self-indulgence, to habits which prevent usefulness and bring misery. Sensual allurements spread snares about their footsteps. They are solicited, upon the right hand and upon the left, to turn aside from the path of patient industry, of persevering study, of sobriety, of virtue, of conscientious obedience to the wishes of parents and the laws of God. Alas! how many listen to the voice of the Tempter, and forego future good for themselves, and blight the hopes of friends, and "bring down gray hairs with sorrow to the grave." Now what the young need to guard them against temptation, to strengthen them in virtue, to nerve their arms for patient and conscientious labor, is that faith of which the apostle speaks, which looks beyond the present, with its pleasures and indulgences, to the future, crowned with results of good or evil, depending upon present choices, and laden with fruits golden as the "apples of the Hesperides," or bitter as those "on the Dead Sea side, all ashes to the taste," — fruits whose seeds are planted by the hands of the young. They need that faith which recognizes an ever-present and all-seeing God, whose perfect law is binding continually upon the heart and the life.

At all ages men are tempted to take a present apparent good, a gratification, an emolument, something which promotes their ease, which increases their wealth, which adds to their power, at the expense of honor, of truth, of right; at the sacrifice of the welfare and happiness of others. And what multitudes yield to this temptation! It is this which causes so many to make shipwreck of personal character; which fills the world with fraud and rapine; which oppresses the hireling in his wages; which wrongs the widow and the orphan; which grinds the face of the poor; which enslaves the bondman; which turns this green earth into a very Aceldama! What is needed is a living faith in the great truth that Jehovah rules in the armies of heaven and among the inhabitants of the earth; that a "Father of the fatherless and a Judge of the widows is God in his holy habitation;" and that, sooner or later, "he abases the proud and lifts up the bowed down." This is the victory that overcometh the world, even our faith.

The hour of sorrow comes. Those

dearer to us than our own life die. Hopes cherished and plans pursued for years are blighted. We stand, stricken and desolate, amid the ruins of all we hold dear. In that dark hour, it is faith in God which overcometh the world and giveth the victory, — that faith which, when it cannot see, sweetly trusts God's wisdom and goodness ; which never doubts his fatherly love and care, and which, the thicker the darkness and the fiercer the storm, but presses closer to the side of him who reveals himself the Elder Brother, the Saviour, and who whispers to such as love him, " Lo, I am with you alway, even unto the end of the world;" "Let not your heart be troubled, neither let it be afraid." Oh, when Christ reveals himself to the heart agitated, distressed, despairing, its sorrows are assuaged, its tumults cease, serenity and peace and calm, hopeful trust, are its portion. Then faith overcometh the world.

Some sharp hour of national trial and conflict arises. Principles are assailed; rights are imperilled; cherished institutions are endangered. Foreign invaders or domestic traitors strike at the very existence of the nation. Now, there is a call of duty. On the one side, plead ease, safety, personal advantage, the emoluments of business. On the other, patriotism, conscience, the preservation of social and civil rights, the defence of institutions purchased by sufferings`and laden with blessings for the race. To determine duty aright there must be an undoubting trust in the power of truth; an assurance, which nothing can shake, in the final triumph of right, because the Almighty is a God of truth and righteousness, and sits sovereign arbiter among the nations. There needs the faith of the Swedish hero, Gustavus Adolphus, who fell on the bloody field of Lutzen, and whose armies went into the battles fought for the Reformation, singing, —

" Fear not; be strong! your cause belongs
   To him who can avenge your wrongs;
      Leave all to him, your Lord:
   Though hidden yet from mortal eyes,
   Salvation shall for you arise:
      He girdeth on his sword!

"As sure as God's own promise stands,
   Not earth nor hell, with all their bands,
      Against us shall prevail:
   The Lord shall mock them from his throne;
   God is with us, we are his own;
      Our victory cannot fail."

Such faith overcometh the world. This animated the breasts of those of whom the apostle writes, " Who through faith subdued kingdoms, wrought righteousness, obtained promises, out of weakness were made strong, waxed valiant in fight, turned to flight the armies of the aliens."

These truths find their illustration in the life and character of one whose early death we mourn, and in the circumstances, private and public, which surround us to-day.

In speaking here of Lieutenant Joseph P. Burrage under the solemnities of the place and of the hour, I but yield to the promptings of my own heart, and pay a deserved though unworthy tribute to a character of rare social and Christian excellence. And you will allow me to say that I speak what

I personally know, for my acquaintance with him was of the most familiar character. During the four years of his college life, there was scarce a week in which he was not at my house. His hopes and wishes and aspirations were perhaps known to me as well as to any one, so that I can speak of him confidently, from an intimate personal acquaintance.

The outward facts of his life are soon stated.

After a quiet and obedient boyhood, he pursued his preparatory studies at Phillips Academy, Andover. In the autumn of Eighteen Hundred and Fifty-eight, he entered Harvard College. In September of the same year, he united with this church, upon a profession of his faith in Christ. In the spring of Eighteen Hundred and Sixty-one, when traitorous hands assailed the institutions of freedom, and the old flag, under which our national glory had been won and our national rights maintained, was shamefully stricken down on Sumter; and especially when the tidings came, which electrified the whole nation, of the cowardly massacre in the streets of Baltimore, his whole soul was stirred within him, and he pondered long and prayerfully the question, whether it was not his duty to join the gathering hosts of the free. With his usual good judgment he came to the conclusion that he ought to complete his college course, and then hold himself in readiness to do whatever his country required at his hand. Accordingly, he remained in the University, and graduated with honor in the class of Eighteen Hundred and Sixty-two. He pronounced an oration at the Commencement exercises on Wednesday. On Saturday of the same week, he enlisted as a private in the Thirty-third Regiment Massachusetts Volunteers, and on the following Wednesday, one week from his graduation, entered upon his duties in

camp at Lynnfield. Thus at once ex-
changing the ease and dignity of an academic life for the hardships and perils
of a private soldier.

He was immediately appointed a Ser-
geant; was soon after made the Orderly
of the company; and in May last re-
ceived a commission as Second Lieutenant. All who knew him felt that his
promotion was fairly and honorably won,
and was but the earnest of still higher
honors. Indeed, his captain writes, that
had he survived the engagement in
which he fell, he would at once have
been promoted.

His regiment, for a few months, did

duty as provost-marshal's guard at Alexandria, and then joined the Army of the Potomac, with which it remained nearly a year, sharing its vicissitudes.

The Thirty-third bore its part in the bloody but fruitless battle of Chancellorsville. It participated in the long and exhausting marches which attended the concentration of our troops at Gettysburg, and shared the perils and the honors of that glorious day, which turned back the thwarted and discomfited hosts of Rebellion.

After the disaster at Chickamauga, it was sent to reinforce the imperilled Army of the Cumberland. On the evening of the 28th of October, the regiment, wearied with the fatigues and hardships of a long passage, reached Brown's Ferry, in the vicinity of Chattanooga, Tennessee, and encamped with the hope of an unbroken night's rest.

It was soon discovered, however, that the rebels had obtained possession of a hill, near Lookout Mountain, which commanded the road and the railway, — thus virtually separating two corps of the army. It was necessary they should be dislodged. They were evidently in force, carefully intrenched. The sides of the hill were abrupt, in many places precipitous. To assail them was a work of difficulty and peril. But, at all hazards, it must be done. So, at midnight, the weary Thirty-third, just beginning to taste the sweets of repose, were called out. Willingly they obeyed the summons, and sprang to arms. In the bright moonlight, the brigade was formed; the Thirty-third Massachusetts and Seventy-third Ohio in the advance, the One Hundred and Thirty-sixth New York and Fifty-fifth Ohio as a support. At the word of command, with a cheer which echoed along the rocky heights " the battle-cry of freedom," they moved forward. As they clambered up the steep ascent, the light of that full October moon made them but too visible marks for the foe. Yet, with fixed bayonets, faltering not in their perilous work, on they went, with repeated charges, in the face of rifle-pits and breast-works blazing with murderous fire, till the routed enemy, who outnumbered the storming party three to one, were driven in confusion from their strong-holds. The success was rapid, — the achievement brilliant. Colonel Under-wood writes that the Massachusetts Thir-ty-third that night won the applause of the veteran army of the Cumberland.

But, ah! how much was crowded into that brief hour's strife! The assault, the fierce rattle of musketry, the bloody charge with the bayonet, the shout, the groan, the wounded, the dying, the dead! And when the brief struggle was over, two-thirds the way up the ascent, falling in the second charge while cheering on his men, lay peacefully—wrapped around with the soft, white moonlight, as if shrouded for his burial by angelic hands — that youthful form, tenderly nurtured, over which scarce twenty-one years had passed, least fitted of all, it would seem to us, for scenes of strife and blood. In his early prime, on that distant battle-field, struck by a ball which broke the stem of his watch and pierced his heart, our young brother fell, a martyr to his country. With no suffering, caught up almost as in a chariot of fire like the prophet from the plain of Jordan, he in a moment exchanged hardship, peril, anxiety, strife, for rest, peace, joy. One moment, the roar of battle; the next, the "song of Moses and the Lamb." Young, pure, patriotic, Christian, he laid himself a willing sacrifice upon the altar of Liberty. Among the thousands of the pure and noble dead, none purer, few nobler than he. He had learned, on the classic page he loved so well, that "it is sweet and fitting to die for one's country;" and the gospel had taught him, in defence of truth and right, not to count his life dear unto him; and he willingly gave it to his native land.

Another is added to the list of the fallen, whose names a grateful country will not willingly let die. And, dear friends, the roll of our own martyred dead is lengthening out,—Ingalls, Locke, Brooks, Clarke, Kenny, Hill, Frost, Burrage,—we honor them all. And it is meet that those nurtured amid historic scenes, upon soil which drank the first blood of the Revolution, within sight of the graves where sleeps the sacred dust of heroes stricken on the fated day of Lexington and Concord, should answer to the call of freedom, if need be with their lives.

Standing over these remains, I have no wish to speak mere words of eulogy. We "come to bury, not to praise." Yet Lieutenant Burrage had characteristics of so marked and special excellence that they deserve more specific statement here.

He had great simplicity of character. He put on no airs. He made no pretensions. He was no boaster. Even his family friends knew of some college honors only when they were announced in the papers or mentioned by others. He was thoroughly honest, transparent as crystal. What he was, you saw and knew. There was no attempt at concealment or double-dealing. In this lay .one great charm of his character, — his naturalness and guilelessness, his unaffected modesty and truthfulness.

He had, too, great kindness of heart. No one was readier than he to do a favor, and to do it without seeming to impose an obligation. While in college, — what most young men would have felt beneath them, — he would come daily and sit by the bedside of an invalid much younger than himself, to lighten and cheer the loneliness of the sick room. Indeed, he bore that severe test of true kindness of heart, the judgment of children. He was a favorite with them. He was greatly esteemed in the families with which he was intimate. In at least three households the remark has been made in my hearing, "No one could have died, outside of our family circle, whom we should miss so much as Joseph."

At home, he was always a dutiful and affectionate son and brother. We admired the mingled delicacy and manliness with which he bore himself toward one with whom he was brought into new and intimate home-relations; and the grief, like that of a mother for her own child, which follows the sundering of these recently-formed ties, is an impressive testimonial to his worth.

This young friend of ours was remarkably pure-minded. I think the instances are exceedingly rare of a young man spending eight years in public institutions, surrounded by men of all grades of moral character, exposed to subtle yet powerful temptation, subject to tests of virtuous principle under which multitudes fail, yet preserving such purity of mind and purity of heart as he. He came out from college, — where many become really corrupted, and a larger number put on the airs of men of the world, — as the three young Jews did from the furnace of the Babylonian king, "upon whose bodies the fire had no power, nor was a hair of their head singed, neither were their coats changed, nor had the smell of fire passed on them."

Lieutenant Burrage was faithful to all his duties. This was so in college; he rarely missed an exercise. It was so as a scholar and teacher in the Sabbath school; he was always punctual, always prepared. He was seldom absent from the prayer-meeting; but was ready to stand in his place and do his part. He exhibited the same faithfulness to duty in the army. His captain writes thus to his father: "You have lost a noble son and the country a noble soldier. He was a good officer. He was strictly conscientious in his duties, and was beloved by all in the company and the regiment. While mourning his loss, you have the satisfaction of knowing that he died a Christian." And two privates in the company of which he was so long Orderly, and who are present at these services to-day, bear witness to his faithfulness and his impartiality. Wherever he was, he had an earnest desire to be useful. He strove to do good while with us and when separated from us. I have recently seen a most touching letter to a young friend, dated but a few months ago, urging an immediate attention to personal religion. We have listened to his letters from the army addressed to the Sabbath school, entreating its members to come to Christ. Even the benevolent collections of the church were not forgotten; but he wrote his father to contribute for him of the money he had sent home.

Lieutenant Burrage, to a degree which few of any age are, was conscientious. He acted from a sense of duty, because the action was *right* and he *ought* to do it. This was eminently shown in his enlisting. He, tenderly brought up, accustomed to refined society, fond of books, with all the associations of academic life fresh upon him, enlisted as a private soldier, to endure labors and hardships and perils, which he must share with a multitude of others, and in which he could scarcely hope to find distinction. He knew what he must meet. He counted the cost. His act was from no transient excitement, no love of novelty, no restless desire of change; but from the stern convictions of duty. He saw the crime of this great treason. He recognized the claims which his country, in the hour of her peril, has upon her sons. He believed that God's voice called him to the field of strife. And so, calmly, resolutely, unflinchingly, with the courage of a hero and the faith of a martyr, he entered upon that path which proved, alas! but a short road to the tomb. His conscientiousness was carried into all his relations to his fellow-men and to his God. His moral and religious character was untarnished even by the breath of suspicion.

Now let it be said to the young here, to all, this character of him whose death we mourn, — his purity, his faithfulness, his conscientiousness, his Christian integrity, — are an illustration of the text, and led to its choice. "This is the victory that overcometh the world, even our faith." It was his confidence in truth, in God, in the final triumph of right, which made him what he was. He was subject to the same temptations to idleness, to sensual indulgences, to take present gratifications instead of future good, to which others are exposed. But he had "faith," and it gave him the "victory." He believed there was something higher, purer, better, nobler, than present indulgence; and that was truth, duty, usefulness, love to God and obedience to his law. He remembered that "The things which are seen are temporal, while the things which are unseen are eternal." And so, when temptations assailed, when evil influences were about him, when godless companions sought to lead him astray, this was the victory which overcame the world, even his faith. And his letters from the army, breathing as they do a deeply-religious spirit, show that there, amid all the surrounding defilements, he kept his robes clean and walked "as seeing Him who is invisible."

It is sad to see one so pure, so conscientious, so desirous of usefulness, cut off in the morning of his days. It is a loss to the country, a loss to the world, a loss especially to this community; and the presence here to-day of the authorities of the town, and of this large audience, proves that the loss is deeply felt. Yet let us not say that he lived in vain. His life is no unfinished fragment, to be symbolized at his grave by a broken column. We are not compelled to turn away from his life-work as from something just begun and then left incomplete forever.

Look at what he accomplished. In a few brief years he developed a personal character of rare beauty. He wrought carefully his own spirit. It was God's most precious gift. He recognized its worth, and strove to make it what the Master would approve. He sought diligently to fit it for the Lord's hand, " in that day when he maketh up his jewels." And that work of mental and spiritual culture, that process of growth and development, commenced here, shall be carried on, under more favorable conditions, and with constantly enlarging powers, forever.

He was a constant comfort and blessing, while he lived, to all with whom he was intimately associated; and his memory is embalmed in their hearts, and they will cherish it ever as a precious legacy.

Then he was permitted, for more than a year, to assist in defending and maintaining the endangered institutions of his country. They were dear to him. He was ready to hazard all he loved in their support. And, ah, at what a price are they being preserved! These thousands of precious lives! And yet, are not these great interests of freedom, of humanity, of religion, worth what their preservation costs? Who shall estimate the value of that which is at stake in this contest? And the name of each one who, in a spirit of true patriotism, gives himself to the service of his country shall be imperishably associated with its redemption. If he live, we will pay him the tribute of our praise, and will teach our children to revere him; and if he fall, his grave shall be but the bed of honor. With the patriotic and immortal dead our young brother now sleeps.

Oh, say not that his life was in vain! Say not that the hopes and aspirations of years have been all defeated! He still lives! Lives in the beauty of his example, in the purity of his influence: lives in the hearts of those who loved him, and who will be strengthened against temptation and stimulated to duty by the remembrance of what he was: lives in the very perpetuity of the institutions he died to save: lives in that immortal life on high.

Four years ago, in the dark, silent hours of a December night, a devoted Christian wife and mother lay breathing out her life. As a few of us surrounded her death-bed, she spoke calmly, trustingly, with holy peace, of her wishes for her children. Her thoughts dwelt upon her first-born. "Joseph — yes, Joseph must be a missionary." Ah, little thought that dying mother, little thought that weeping boy, who hid his face in her pillow, what his mission was to be!

Amid the perils of civil war, to defend the rights of freedom; on the field of conflict, to lay down his young life! But, if it be indeed allowed the departed still to take cognizance of those they love on earth, and to be "ministering spirits, sent to minister unto such as are heirs of salvation,"—if it be, who shall say that in the camp, or on the march, or in the hour of peril, that mother did not watch over him as lovingly and approvingly as if he had been laboring for Christ on the plains of India or amid the islands of the Pacific waste? And who shall say that she did not greet his freed spirit, going up from that field of midnight strife on the banks of the Tennessee, with as holy joy and as approving welcome as if it had ascended from the shores of the Ganges or the Nile? And may we not believe that as the young soldier, his armor just laid aside, bowed himself before the throne of God and of the Lamb, it was said to him, as to any fallen missionary of the cross, "WELL DONE, GOOD AND FAITHFUL SERVANT; THOU HAST BEEN FAITHFUL OVER A FEW THINGS; ENTER THOU INTO THE JOY OF THY LORD."